TWENTY THOUSAND LEAGUES UNDER THE SEA

Library of Congress Cataloging-in-Publication Data

James, Raymond.
Twenty thousand leagues under the sea / by Jules Verne; retold by Raymond James; illustrated by Wayne Geehan.
p. cm.
Summary: An adaptation for a young audience of the nineteenth-century tale of an electric submarine, its eccentric captain, and the undersea world, which anticipated many of the scientific achievements of the twentieth century.
ISBN 0-8167-1879-2 (lib. bdg.) ISBN 0-8167-1880-6 (pbk.)
[1. Sea stories—Fiction. 2. Submarines—Fiction. 3. Science fiction.]
I. Geehan, Wayne, ill. II. Verne, Jules, 1828-1905. Vingt mille lieues sous les mers. III. Title.
PZ7.J1543Tw 1990
[Fic]—dc20 89-34248

Printed in the United States of America.
10 9 8 7 6 5 4 3 2 1

TWENTY THOUSAND LEAGUES UNDER THE SEA

JULES VERNE

Retold by
Raymond James

Illustrated by
Wayne Geehan

Troll Associates

"We're sinking! We're sinking!"

There was a gaping hole in the ship *Scotia* about two yards wide. The ocean was pouring through it.

The captain remembered a sharp jolt some seconds earlier, but had thought nothing of it at the time. Sturdily built, the *Scotia* was miles from any rocks or land masses.

Several yards below the ship's water line was a hole in the shape of a near perfect triangle. Whatever hit the *Scotia* was obviously powerful.

The *Scotia* was only one of many ships that were struck by this strange force in 1867. Newspaper reports said that it was long and spindle-shaped and that it gave off an eerie light in the water. Whether it was animal, sea monster, or machine—no one could tell.

I read these newspaper reports in New York. My friend, Conseil, and I had just returned from the Nebraska badlands where we had done some scientific research. We were hoping to leave New York on the next ship back to France. There, as a professor at Paris' Museum of Natural History, I planned to write a book on my scientific findings. An earlier book I had written, *Mysteries of the Depths of the Sea,* had established me as an expert on life in the ocean.

So I must admit that these stories about the ''sea monster'' aroused my curiosity. From the accounts I read, I thought it was one of two things: a powerful underwater machine or a mammal of enormous strength. Most likely, it was a gigantic narwhal. This whale has a long ivory spike to attack and kill other whales. I said as much to the newspaper reporters who asked me to comment on the matter. And they quoted me, ''Professor Pierre Aronnax,'' in their headline stories the next day.

Still, fear continued to spread. Before long, a frigate of great speed and strength, the *Abraham Lincoln,* was outfitted and armed to chase the creature.

Just three hours before the frigate was scheduled to depart, I received a telegram from the U.S. Secretary of the Navy. He had read the news stories quoting my opinion, and asked that I join the expedition and provide scientific advice. Without delay, Conseil and I took our already packed bags and headed for the pier.

MARINE LIFE

The *Abraham Lincoln* ran at full steam in the Atlantic. We would travel south to the tip of South America and come up into the Pacific. There, in the north, between the eastern coast of Japan and the western coast of the United States, we hoped to meet the creature.

Among the crew members was Ned Land, whose skill with a harpoon was unmatched. Though he had a bold look about him, he spoke very little.

The voyage was mostly peaceful. The only excitement was when Ned helped an American whaling ship catch a particularly large whale it was chasing. With one fearsome plunge of his harpoon, Ned struck the whale straight to the heart!

For three months, the *Abraham Lincoln* explored the waters of the northern Pacific. We were now just two hundred miles off the coast of Japan. Trailing behind the ship were large slabs of bacon dangled as bait for the creature. But only the sharks seemed interested. The creature had not appeared, and the men were getting restless.

"Look out there!" shouted Ned Land from the bow one day. "It's the very thing we're after!"

All of us ran to the railing where Ned was pointing out to sea. There, no more than five hundred yards away, a brilliant light shone beneath the waves. It moved with incredible speed, rushing toward us, then veering off to the side. It flashed toward us once more, this time stopping just twenty feet from our hull before fading away again.

The captain approached me. "Wouldn't you say, Professor Aronnax, that we're dealing with a giant narwhal?"

I nodded my head in agreement, though the unusual light of the animal made me hesitate.

The creature did not appear again that day. But neither crew nor captain slept that night. Everyone was awake in the darkness. What *were* we dealing with?

At about one o'clock in the morning, I heard a deafening roar. Conseil, Ned, and I quickly climbed to the deck and found the captain already there. His eyes squinted as he tried to peer into the darkness.

"Mr. Land, did that sound like the roar of a whale to you?" asked the captain.

"Could be, Captain," replied Ned. "I'd like to get within striking distance of it with my harpoon."

All of us stayed on deck and kept watch. Hours went by. Then traces of sunlight glinted over the eastern horizon. The morning fog drifted in. It would be daybreak soon. Perhaps then we'd be able to see this creature that bellowed in the night.

Suddenly, around mid-morning, we saw a long, black body about a mile and a half from the frigate. I estimated the length of the creature to be about 250 feet. It sprayed two jets of water straight up into the air, rising over a hundred feet.

"Put on all steam!" the captain commanded. "Make straight for that creature, men!"

The crew cheered and dashed to their posts on deck. With a full head of steam, the *Abraham Lincoln* plowed directly at the beast. But it always managed to stay just out of reach. No matter how fast the frigate went, the creature easily eluded her. The captain was clearly frustrated.

"Mr. Land," he said, "should we put out the boats to give chase?"

"No, sir," Ned said grimly. "That devil won't be taken so easily. But if you can get up more steam, I may be able to harpoon it."

"Go forward, then, Mr. Land," said the captain. "Engineer, give us more steam!"

The swiftest ship in the U.S. Navy was now at full throttle. It could not go any faster. Yet the creature remained out of reach. The crew began cursing at the beast.

"Man the guns!" the captain ordered. "We'll see if this beast can outrun cannon shot!"

The men obeyed the command. Soon, shot after shot boomed out. But each one merely glanced off the rounded surface of the animal. What beast could repel flying lead? I wondered. Clearly, this was an animal of almost supernatural strength and quickness!

For hours, the frigate rained cannon shots at the beast. But they had no effect. And even more amazing was the energy of the animal—it never seemed to tire. Night came on again, and the frigate was no closer to catching her prey than the day before.

Suddenly, a glow appeared on the ocean's surface a hundred feet from the *Abraham Lincoln*. Silently, the ship drew near it. I stood by the railing with Conseil. Closer and closer we came. Ned had his harpoon ready. Twenty feet from the creature, Ned reared back and with all his might threw his harpoon. It hit with a metallic clink. The creature's light vanished. Then two enormous waterspouts broke over the railing of the ship. I saw Ned Land tumble into the ocean—and I went with him.

"Help! Help!" I shouted, hoping the crew of the *Abraham Lincoln* would hear me. Then, as my mouth filled with seawater, a strong hand seized me and lifted me up. It was Conseil!

"Lean on my shoulder, Professor," said Conseil. "You'll swim more easily."

"What about the frigate?"

"The frigate?" said Conseil, stroking in the water. "Just before I dove in for you, I heard the men at the wheel say the rudder and the propeller were broken."

"Broken?" I asked, surprised.

"Yes, broken—by the monster's teeth! It's bad luck for us."

"Then we're lost!" I exclaimed.

The moon broke through the clouds overhead. In the pale light shining on the water, Conseil and I could see the *Abraham Lincoln* in the distance. We shouted at it for help, even though we knew our cries couldn't be heard. Then, a hard body struck me. I clung to it. In a moment, it was raising me above the surface of the water. But I collapsed from fatigue, and fainted.

On waking, I looked up and saw a familiar face gazing down at me. "Ned!" I cried. "Is it you?"

"It is, Professor," the harpooner replied. "I was luckier than you and Conseil. I found my footing on a floating island."

"An island?" I blurted.

"Well, actually more like an iron beast. That's why my harpoon never entered its skin. It's this beast we ride on now." There could be no doubt about it. We were on the back of some sort of submarine!

"As long as it sails on the surface," said Ned, "we'll be all right. But if it takes a fancy to dive, I wouldn't give two straws for our lives."

A bubbling began at the rear of the vessel. We were now moving on the surface. If we could hold on until morning, I reasoned, we might yet survive.

Daybreak came. The morning mists engulfed us and the vessel. And Ned could contain his patience no longer.

"Confound it, open up!" he shouted, kicking one of the plates on the vessel's back. "Open up, you coldhearted rascals!"

With that, an iron plate was pushed aside from underneath. Then, eight strong men seized all three of us and dragged us below into the belly of the beast.

We were plunged into darkness. A few uneasy hours passed. Then a door swung open and a light shone. A man gave us dry clothes. Another man, tall, with a large forehead and large black eyes, stood back in the doorway. Judging by his clean, almost noble appearance, I took him for the commander of this vessel. I told him who we were and what had happened to us. But he didn't seem the slightest bit interested. He left, then another man who must have been the steward came and laid out a meal for us on a table.

We ate fish of all descriptions. And each fork, spoon, knife, and plate had a large N engraved on it. What did it mean? That was the question I asked myself as my two companions and I drifted off into a deep sleep.

Ned Land awoke first. And when the door swung open again, he lunged at the steward bringing us breakfast. The harpooner had him by the throat on the floor. Conseil and I, startled by the noise, rushed over and tried to pry Ned off. A voice boomed at us from the doorway.

"Stop, Master Land!"

It was the same tall man who had appeared the previous day. He was plainly in command of this vessel, and he watched us with calm attention. Ned removed his hands from the steward's throat.

"Professor Aronnax, will you be so kind as to listen to me?" he said. "I could have spoken earlier, but I first wanted to observe you. Now I have."

All three of us were surprised by the easy confidence of the man. I was about to speak up when he waved his hand for silence.

"Fate has brought you into the presence of someone who has broken all ties to mankind," he said, referring to himself. "You were aboard a ship that attacked this one. By rights, I should treat you as enemies. I could place you on the deck of this ship, plunge it beneath the waters, and forget you ever existed. Again, that would be my right."

Here I interrupted. "Sir, that might be the right of a savage, but not that of a civilized man!"

"Civilized?" he snorted in reply. "Professor, I am done with what you call 'civilization.' And I am done with its laws. I answer only to myself, my own laws, for under the sea *I* am master."

The fire in his eyes told me he would not be argued with. I stayed silent as he continued.

"You are here at my whim. You will be allowed to move freely within this ship. In exchange for this liberty, you will obey one condition. There will be times when I must confine you to your quarters. And you must obey me. Do you accept this condition?"

"We accept," I answered for all of us.

Ned Land shook his head. "I will never give my word of honor not to try to escape," he said defiantly.

"I did not ask for your word of honor on that, Master Land," replied the commander coldly. "I ask only that you obey my order to stay in your quarters when I deem it necessary." Then he looked at all three of us. "You are going to see things only I and the men on board my *Nautilus* have seen. Marvels of nature, secrets of the deep. Obey—and learn!"

"And by what name," I asked, "should we address you, commander?"

His eyes became slits. "I am nothing to you but Captain Nemo. And you are nothing to me but passengers aboard the *Nautilus*." He turned and left the cabin, leaving the three of us behind, stunned.

In the days and weeks that followed, I explored the *Nautilus* from stem to stern. It had a huge library, crammed with thousands of scientific books, including my own. The ship also had a museum. It contained priceless paintings as well as fossils and shells and pieces of coral too beautiful to describe. And in a separate compartment were pearls that dazzled the eye. Some were as big as grapefruit!

The ship itself was even more amazing than the precious cargo it carried. It was powered by electricity, and various instruments to measure depth and temperature and oxygen supply hung from the wall. The hull of the *Nautilus* was actually two. It had an inner hull made of steel plates two and a half inches thick. The outer hull was ten inches thick.

Off to one side of the deck, in a shallow indent, I could see a small boat bolted in place. I asked the captain about this. His reply was curt. "Just a small craft for convenience, Professor. Or for emergencies."

In the forward part of the ship was a steering section. It looked out through specially made glass that could withstand the water pressure. At the very front of the ship was a pointed, hard steel snout with a spike. A light swept in front of it. The light came from a huge reflecting disc. Without doubt, the *Nautilus* was the most remarkable vessel yet created by man!

Ned Land, however, was not quite so taken with the ship or with the underwater view it provided. "Professor Aronnax, how many men are there on board? Ten, twenty, fifty, a hundred?" he asked.

"I cannot answer you, Ned," I said. "It's better to bide your time and abandon for now any idea of seizing the vessel or escaping from it. Just watch the extraordinary sight before you!" I gestured toward the brightly colored fish swimming outside the glass.

"We're prisoners in this ship," Ned said. "No amount of 'freedom' on board will change that."

I confess there was truth in what Ned said. But then my eyes wandered out through the glass again, and all thoughts of imprisonment left me.

A few days later, I received an invitation from Captain Nemo to explore the forests of the island of Crespo. I was grateful for the chance to set foot once more on dry land. Little did I know that the forests Captain Nemo was referring to were on the bottom of the sea!

I was summoned to a sealed chamber where I saw Captain Nemo and a few crew men dressing in the oddest clothes. They put on heavy, waterproof suits made of rubber, thick boots, and metal helmets with three separate glass panes for vision.

Once dressed, we strapped metal cylinders of compressed air to our backs in order to breathe. Then Captain Nemo issued all of us a waterproof lantern, charged by electricity, to light our way. We were also given strange guns that could shoot underwater bullets that gave off a powerful electric shock.

I waited with the others until water hissed through a door that had just been slowly opened. Once the chamber we were in had been completely flooded, we stepped out onto the ocean floor. Rocks, shells, fish, and flowers gleamed in the light cast by our lanterns.

Soon I could see ahead of us a dark, bulky mass—the forests of the island of Crespo. When we entered them, I realized they were actually thick clusters of very tall shrubs. Their leaves extended like a canopy up and over our heads, pitching us into shadows streaked with rays of sunlight from above. I felt as if I were sleepwalking, so beautiful and dreamy were these underwater forests.

I snapped to attention, however, when I saw something just to the side of me. Perched on a shrub and about to spring at me was a monstrous sea spider. It was over three feet tall, and its horrible claws were open, ready for the kill. I barely had time to react and defend myself when Captain Nemo struck the spider with the butt end of his gun. It writhed in agony to the sandy floor, its claws tossing wildly.

I motioned to Captain Nemo that I had quite enough of this exploration and wished to return to the *Nautilus*. He understood me and waved all of us back. The closer we came to the ship, the better I was feeling. But suddenly, Captain Nemo dropped flat on the sand, gesturing for the rest of us to do the same. We got down not a moment too soon. Two huge shapes were swimming straight for us. My blood froze in my veins. It was a pair of enormous sharks! Only their poor eyesight saved us, for they swam directly over our heads. A cold, clammy sweat broke out on my forehead inside my helmet. That was too close for comfort!

The *Nautilus* changed course, traveling underwater in a southwesterly direction. Ned, Conseil, and I had been aboard for two months now and had logged over eleven thousand miles. Most of that was underwater.

Moving with breathtaking speed, the *Nautilus* soon approached the dangerous reef of the Coral Sea off the northeast coast of Australia. The reef's coral ridges could cut and gouge any wooden vessel. But the steel hull of the *Nautilus* cruised through without mishap.

Two days later, we sighted the Papuan Islands. It was Captain Nemo's intention to pass them by and travel through the Torres Straits. The sea was rough and battered us on all sides. Still, we got through the straits, then followed a course around the island of Gilboa. The ship was just two miles away from the island when a shock knocked me to the floor.

I ran up on deck. Conseil and Ned quickly joined me. We could see that the *Nautilus* had run aground. It was stuck on top of a coral reef shelf, and the low tide made retreat impossible. We would have to wait until high tide came that evening.

When Captain Nemo appeared on deck, Ned asked permission for the three of us to go ashore. We hoped to use the small boat bolted down to the side of the *Nautilus*. To our surprise, Captain Nemo agreed. Within an hour, the three of us were away in the boat. We carried hatchets and regular guns.

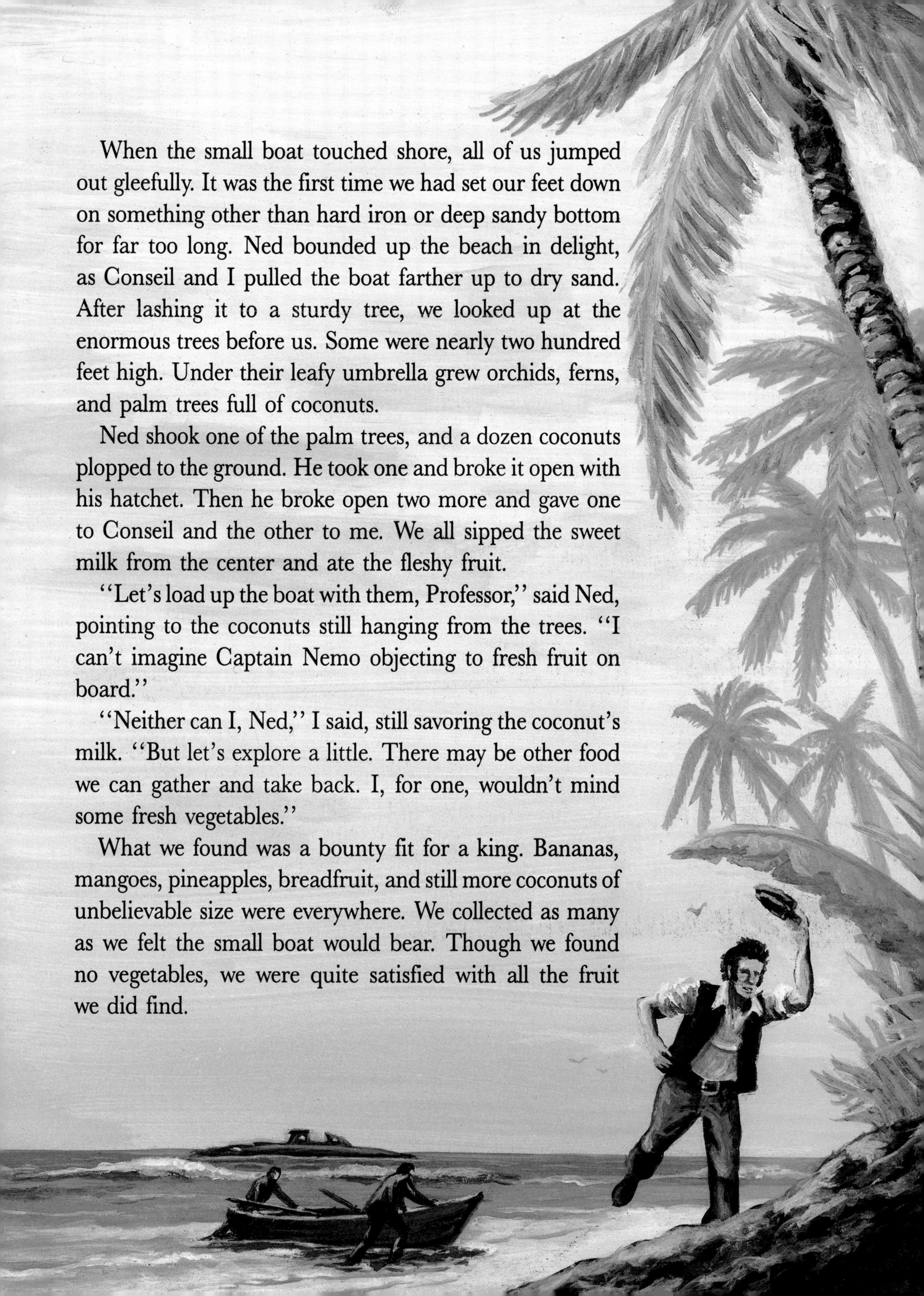

When the small boat touched shore, all of us jumped out gleefully. It was the first time we had set our feet down on something other than hard iron or deep sandy bottom for far too long. Ned bounded up the beach in delight, as Conseil and I pulled the boat farther up to dry sand. After lashing it to a sturdy tree, we looked up at the enormous trees before us. Some were nearly two hundred feet high. Under their leafy umbrella grew orchids, ferns, and palm trees full of coconuts.

Ned shook one of the palm trees, and a dozen coconuts plopped to the ground. He took one and broke it open with his hatchet. Then he broke open two more and gave one to Conseil and the other to me. We all sipped the sweet milk from the center and ate the fleshy fruit.

"Let's load up the boat with them, Professor," said Ned, pointing to the coconuts still hanging from the trees. "I can't imagine Captain Nemo objecting to fresh fruit on board."

"Neither can I, Ned," I said, still savoring the coconut's milk. "But let's explore a little. There may be other food we can gather and take back. I, for one, wouldn't mind some fresh vegetables."

What we found was a bounty fit for a king. Bananas, mangoes, pineapples, breadfruit, and still more coconuts of unbelievable size were everywhere. We collected as many as we felt the small boat would bear. Though we found no vegetables, we were quite satisfied with all the fruit we did find.

We were still plucking fresh fruit off the trees when we heard a grunt from some nearby bushes. All three of us stood still. Then I picked up a coconut and hurled it into the bushes. Out darted a large hog. It squealed as it ran past us and into the bushes again.

Pulling out his gun, Ned chased the hog, hollering almost as loudly as the frightened animal. Then, Conseil and I heard Ned's gun fire. Seconds later, Ned was walking out of the bushes, dragging the body of the hog behind him.

"Pork chops are on me!" he said, beaming.

We built a fire right on the beach and roasted the hog on a wooden spit. It was an excellent supper of roast pork and fresh fruits. We ate until we could not eat another morsel.

"Suppose we don't return to the *Nautilus,* Professor?" asked Ned, playfully peeling a banana where he lay.

But before I could reply, a stone fell at our feet. Then another fell not far from the first. We looked at them, astonished.

"Wha— " exclaimed Ned, but he didn't have the chance to finish his words. A third stone had knocked the banana right out of his hands.

"Savages!" I shouted, shouldering my gun. Conseil and Ned did likewise. There wasn't a moment to lose. "Quick! To the boat!"

We ran for our lives. Twenty men with painted faces broke into a run after us. They were just a few hundred yards away.

Ned slit the rope tied to the boat. We pulled it quickly into the water and jumped in after it. Furiously, we pulled at the oars. Our muscles ached as we tried to row faster and still faster. There were now a hundred savages waist-deep in the water, hurling stones and shooting arrows at us.

Imagine our surprise when we discovered no one on the deck of the *Nautilus.* Couldn't they see or at least *hear* what was happening? Why weren't Nemo and his crew on deck and firing at these savages? Didn't they care about our lives? *Their* lives?

As soon as we climbed on board, I hurried down the main hatch ladder ahead of my two comrades and raced toward Nemo's cabin. There, I found him peacefully reading.

"Captain!" I shouted. "There's a band of savages out there ready to— "

"Savages, you say?" The amused tone of Nemo's voice only made me angry.

"Yes, SAVAGES! Can't you hear them?" I was puzzled by the captain's lack of interest.

"My, my," he answered. "Well, Professor, let's just wait until high tide tonight. Then we'll be off."

Still fuming, I went to my quarters, slamming the door shut. There I stayed with Ned and Conseil until nightfall.

After finally calming down, I decided to get a breath of fresh air up on deck. But as I gazed out toward shore, I noticed about a dozen huge logs drifting toward the *Nautilus*. A moment later, something whizzed past my shoulder and struck the ship with a clank. Looking down at the object, I saw it was a stone-head arrow. I looked back at these logs and could make out the shapes of men sitting in them. These were no logs, but canoes carrying savages. They were about to attack the *Nautilus*!

I dashed down into the ship and told Captain Nemo what I'd seen. He remained as calm and amused as before.

"At any time now, high tide will lift the ship off the reef and out to sea again," he said to me. "Just be patient, Professor." Then he ordered one of the crew members to reopen all the hatches to take on fresh air before we submerged again.

“Captain, are you mad? The savages are outside right now. Some are already on deck. If you open those hatches, they’ll be down here like a shot!”

“Think so, Professor?” he said in a curious voice. “Why don’t we test your theory.” We both walked to where the main hatch was. It had just been opened.

Immediately, a painted face dipped down briefly into the hole. A second later, a foot stepped onto the top rung of the ladder and a hand gripped the railing. A loud shriek followed, and the savage’s face twisted in pain. He flew back up the hole. Another savage tried the ladder after him and also shrieked in pain. From every open hatch came screams of agony. I looked at Captain Nemo, who was laughing.

“Electricity can work any number of wonders, Professor,” he said, still smiling. “That railing you see there is actually a hard metallic cable that can be instantly charged with electric current. I don’t think we’ll have any more visits from our neighbors on shore.”

Then, all of us on board felt the *Nautilus* rise slightly off the reef. High tide had finally come, and soon we were off again underneath the sea.

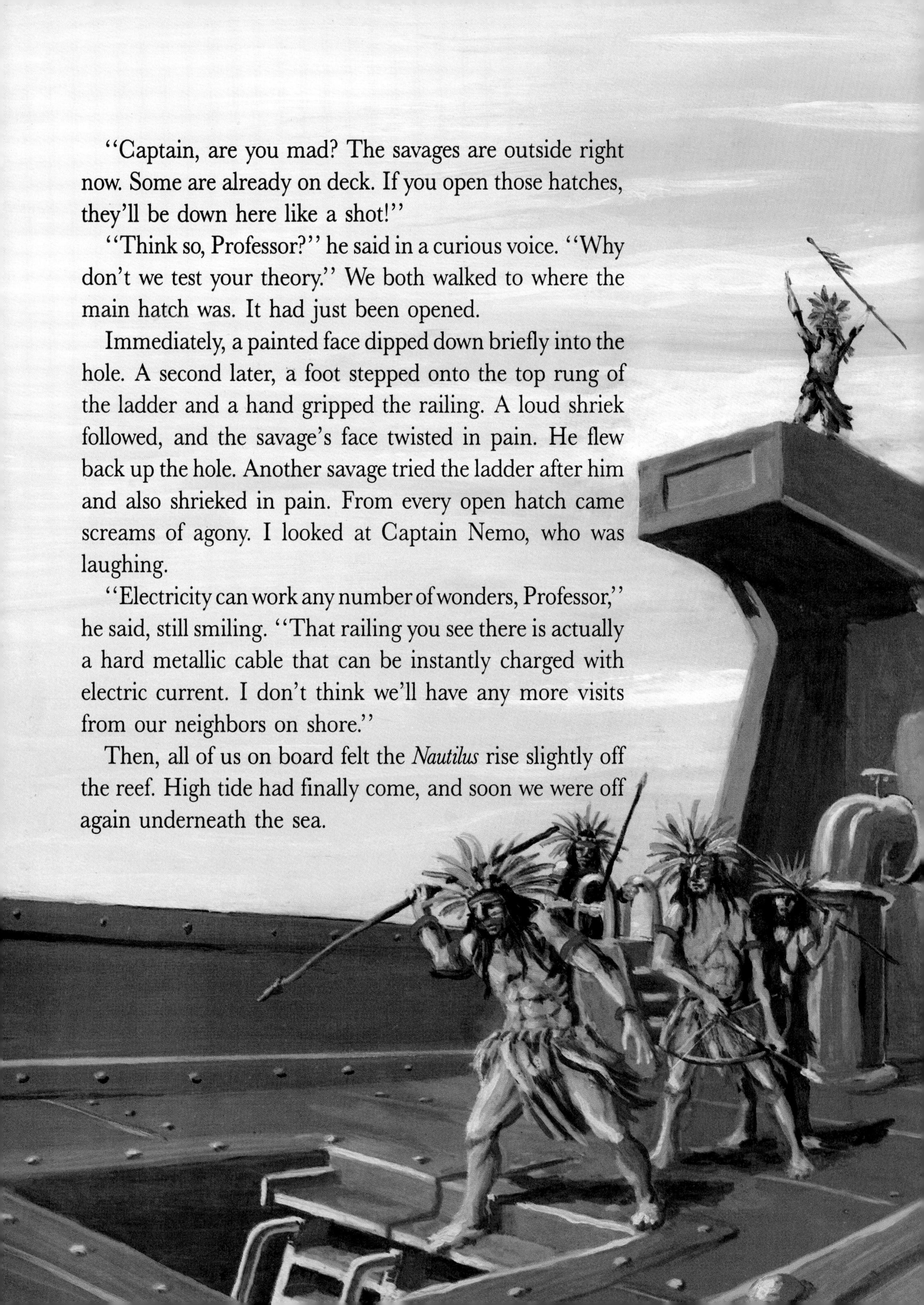

About a week later, Captain Nemo summoned Ned, Conseil, and me to his cabin. He had a grave look on his face.

"Gentlemen, I must ask that you stay confined to your quarters for a while," he said. "I trust you'll remember the condition you agreed to earlier."

With Ned grumbling all the way, the three of us returned to our quarters. A meal awaited us there. As usual, it was delicious. But soon Ned started yawning and finally fell asleep. Conseil's eyelids also began to droop and then close. He, too, was fast asleep now. What was happening? Then I sensed a deep drowsiness coming over me. The food had been drugged! But why? I moved toward the door, slumped down, and blacked out.

We were awakened the next morning by Captain Nemo himself. His eyes were bloodshot and bleary. It was obvious he hadn't slept at all last night. The same grave look was on his face. It was almost sorrowful.

"Professor, are you a surgeon?"

"I have practiced medicine in a hospital," I replied.

"Please come with me," he said, leading me to the crew's quarters.

Lying on a bunk was a man whose head was wound in a thick bandage. It was soaked with blood. I removed the bandage and gaped in horror. The skull had been bored open by some hard, sharp object. The man was dying, and I took the captain aside and told him his crew man was beyond my help.

An hour later, the man died. Captain Nemo led a team of crew members outside the *Nautilus.* They buried their dead comrade in a sandy grave that would eventually be covered by coral. When he returned, Captain Nemo wiped a tear from his eye. It was the first time I ever saw him cry. I knew there was much more to this man than any of us guessed. But not once did he refer to the death or to what caused it.

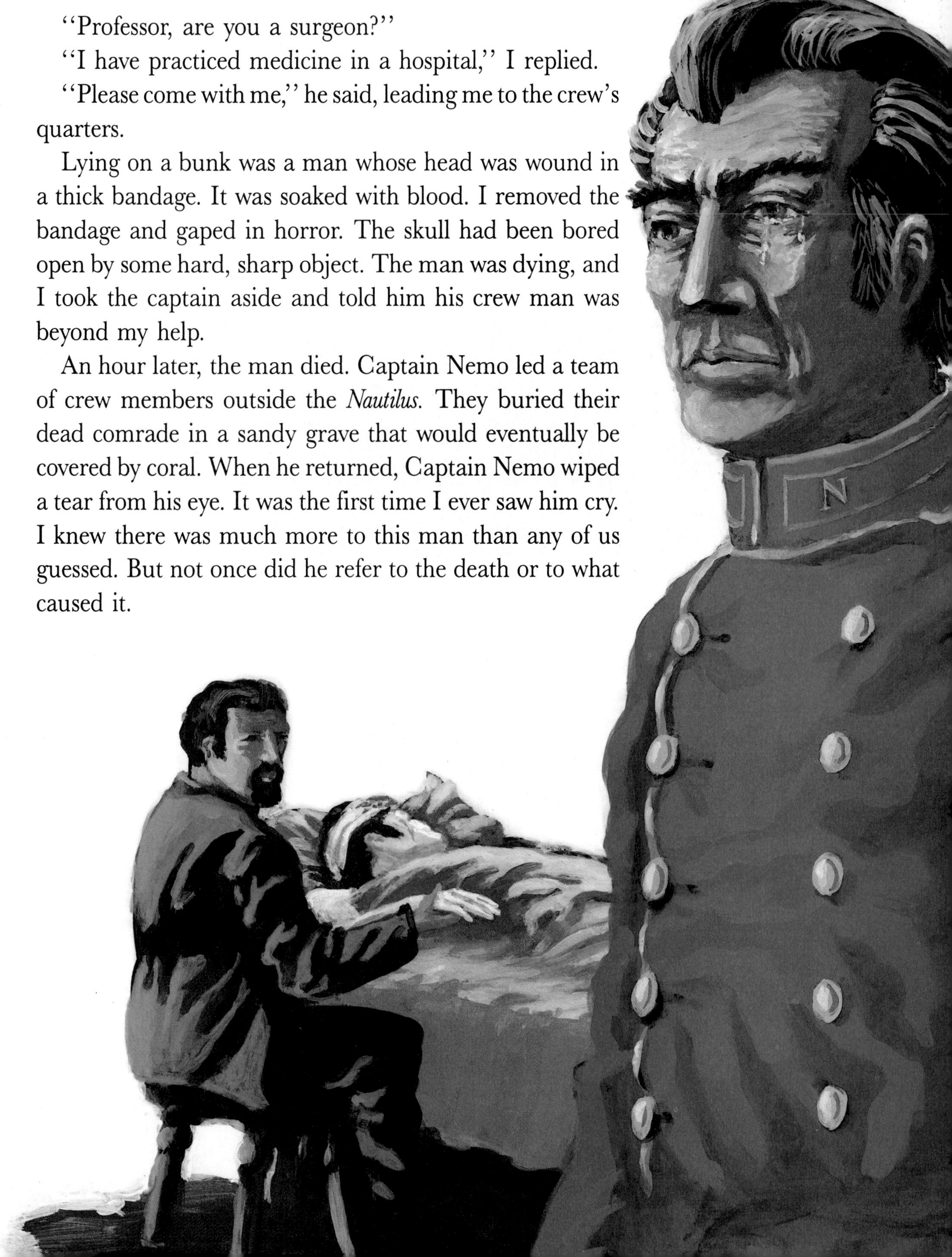

Off the island of Ceylon, the *Nautilus* surfaced. The captain proposed that Conseil, Ned, and I join him and a couple of his men in the small boat. We would explore the famous pearl fisheries just off the coast.

The three of us readily agreed. We dressed in the waterproof suits, put on our metal helmets, and strapped on the oxygen cylinders. We carried only long knives for weapons. Nemo permitted no guns or lanterns this time. But Ned brought along his harpoon as an extra precaution.

It was a bright, sunny afternoon when we reached the underwater oyster beds. On the sandy bottom were oysters of incredible number and size. We pried them open with our knives and filled a few pouches with the pearls we took from inside. Nemo helped us for a while. But then he moved to another location just ahead.

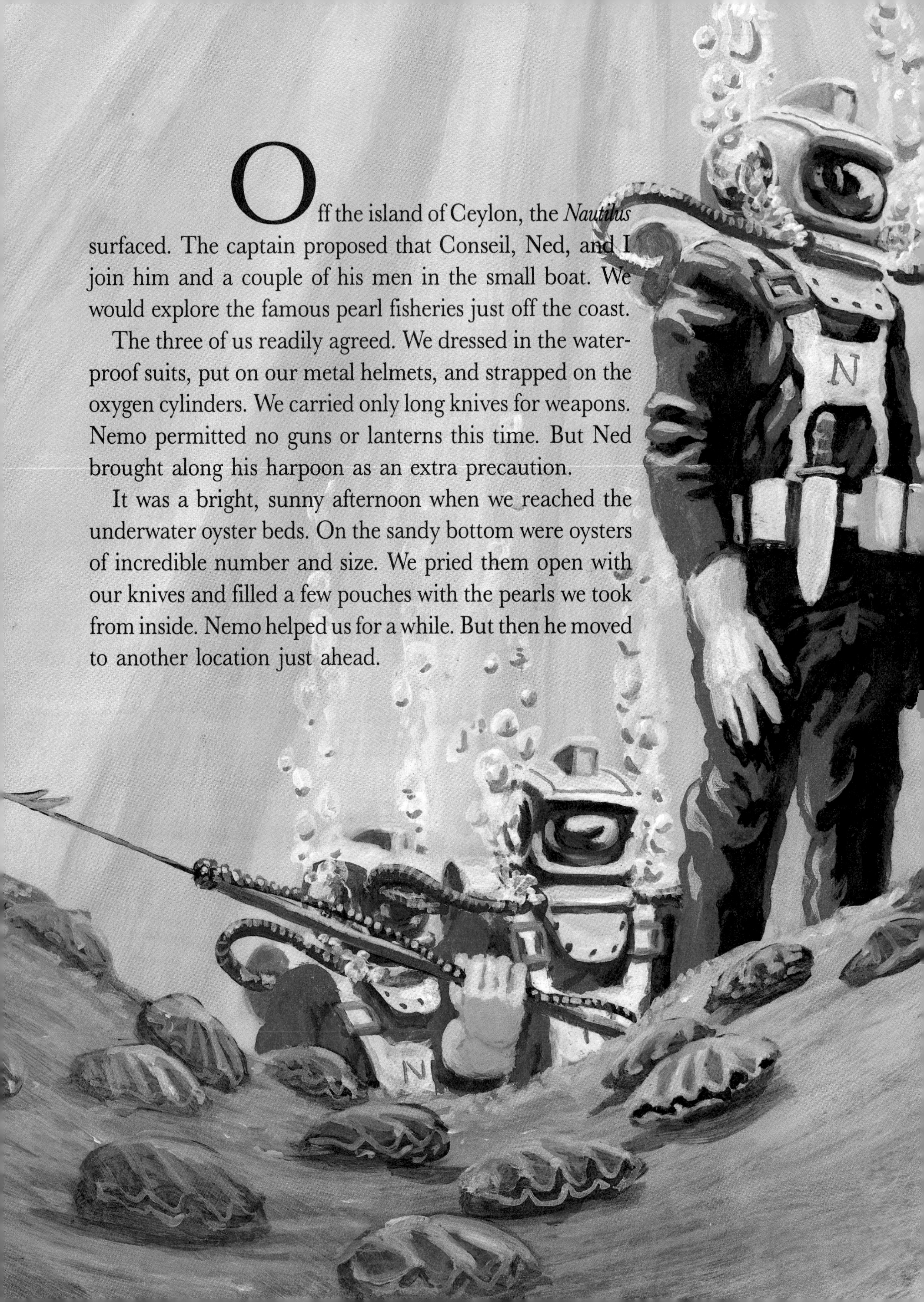

It was a cave. And lying inside it was an enormous oyster, the largest I have ever seen. It must have weighed over six hundred pounds! Using his knife, Nemo pried it open. And there, in the folds of its flesh, was a pearl as big as a coconut. It was a jewel of breathtaking beauty, perfectly round. Its milky color shone in the sunlight cast down from above. But Nemo didn't remove it. Instead, he turned and walked away. It was clear he wanted this giant pearl to grow bigger still, as it had year after year.

Suddenly, Captain Nemo stopped. He signaled to all of us to crouch low behind some rocks. Then, five yards from me, a shadow appeared and sank to the bottom. At first, I thought of sharks. But it was a man, a living man! He dove straight to where the oysters lay, gathered up a handful, and took them back to the surface. I could make out from below the narrow hull of his canoe.

In watching the diver work in the oyster beds, I didn't notice another, much larger shadow racing toward him. It was a mammoth shark! Jaws open, it came right at the diver, who just barely escaped its razor-sharp teeth. But the shark's tail whipped hard against the diver's chest and knocked him to the sand. The shark turned and swam for the diver lying helpless on the bottom. Just then, Captain Nemo leaped from the rocks and buried his knife into the shark's back. Blood gushed from it.

Enraged, the shark came at the captain now. Nemo managed to sidestep its lunge and sink his knife into the shark again. The sea was red, but the shark attacked again. The whip end of its tail caught Captain Nemo across the head. The blow stunned him, leaving him defenseless for a moment. That was enough time for the shark to turn and speed at him for what would surely have been the kill.

The shark's jaws opened and were about to seize the captain at the waist when Ned Land hurled himself forward. With his harpoon, he struck the shark right through its stomach. It thrashed briefly, pouring out thick blood. Then it shivered and died.

Recovering, Captain Nemo went to the diver still lying on the sand and carried him to the surface. In the diver's canoe, all of us worked to revive the man. Finally, he opened his eyes to see four metal helmets peering down at him. He must have thought we were some supernatural creatures from the deep, judging by the wide-eyed stare he gave us. His stare grew even wider when Nemo handed him a pouch full of pearls that we had collected earlier. Without saying so much as goodbye, we plunged over the side of the canoe and returned underwater. Then we started back to the *Nautilus*.

"Thank you, Master Land," said the captain to the harpooner who had just saved his life. Ned nodded. But the distant look in his eye told me he was biding his time. When the right opportunity came along, he would try to leave Nemo and the *Nautilus* once and for all.

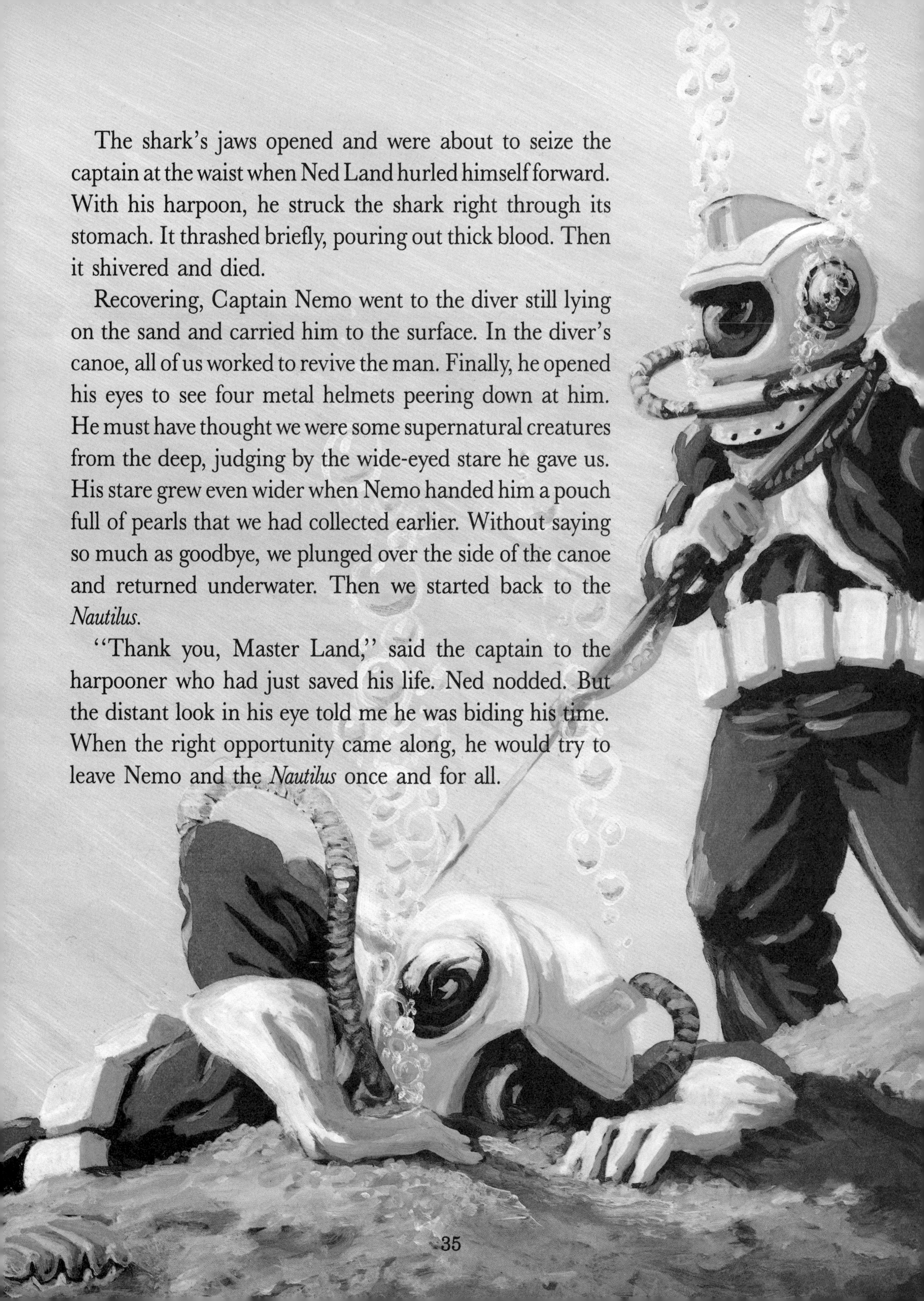

For five months, Ned, Conseil, and I had been passengers on board the *Nautilus*. It was now heading south toward that frigid, desolate continent of Antarctica. Soon we were amid icebergs towering above the ship. The farther south we traveled, the denser and more numerous these icebergs became. It was a dazzling, awesome sight!

The temperature plunged far below zero, but we were all clad in sealskin and fur. The steel spike at the front of the *Nautilus* cut a path through the ice fields. No sooner did we pass through the ice than it closed behind us. At times, I thought we'd be trapped. But the ship proved it could meet the challenge. Like a wedge, it continued moving forward. Nemo was intent on reaching the South Pole!

When the cold became more than we could bear on deck we ducked back inside the ship and fastened all the hatches. Then the *Nautilus* dove beneath the surface to a depth of two thousand feet. We were now traveling under the icebergs. Soon we were under solid ice four hundred yards thick. After a time, as we came closer to the South Pole, the ice above us thinned. Finally, it separated above us, and the ship rose to the surface in one of the clearings.

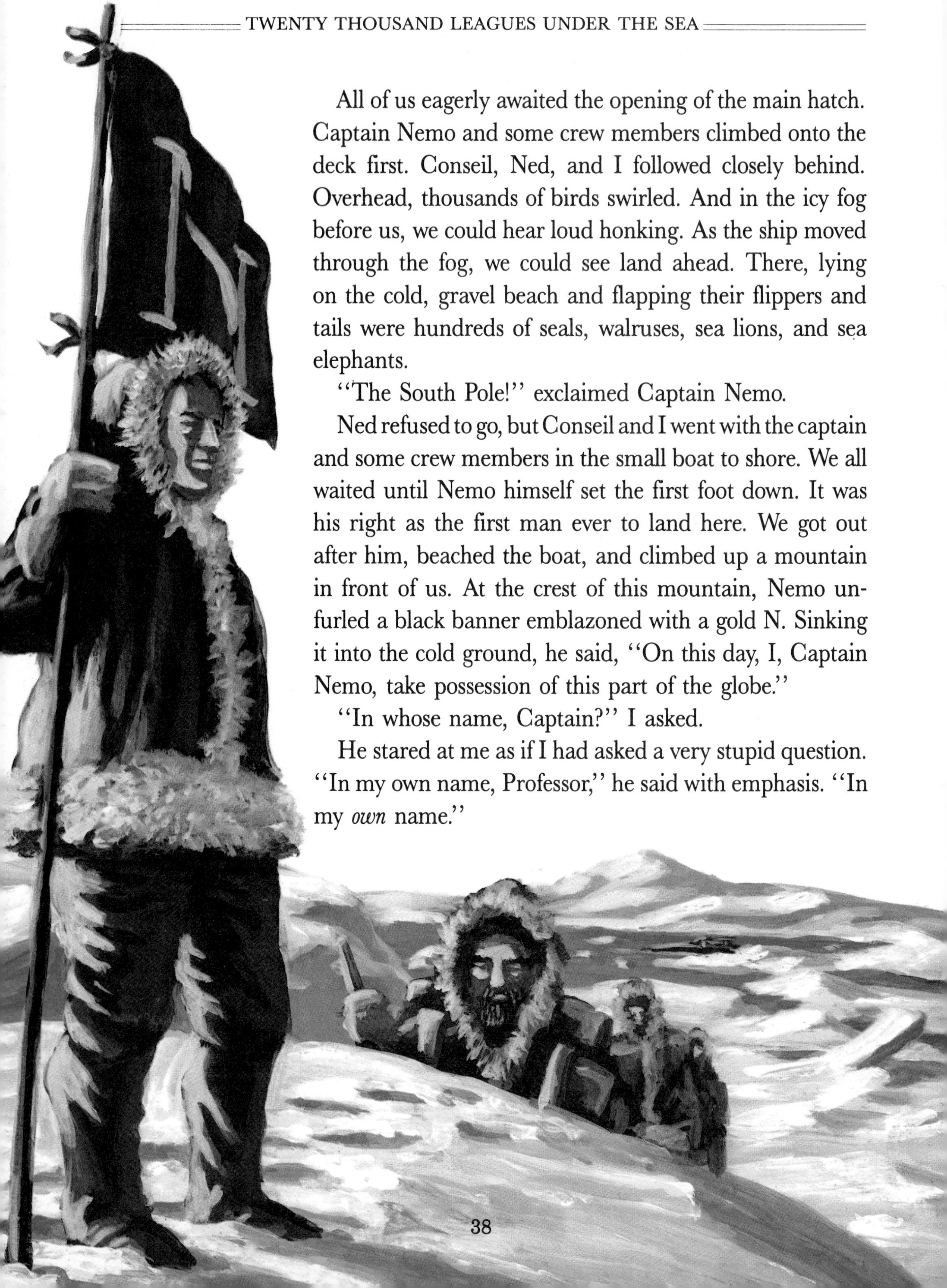

All of us eagerly awaited the opening of the main hatch. Captain Nemo and some crew members climbed onto the deck first. Conseil, Ned, and I followed closely behind. Overhead, thousands of birds swirled. And in the icy fog before us, we could hear loud honking. As the ship moved through the fog, we could see land ahead. There, lying on the cold, gravel beach and flapping their flippers and tails were hundreds of seals, walruses, sea lions, and sea elephants.

"The South Pole!" exclaimed Captain Nemo.

Ned refused to go, but Conseil and I went with the captain and some crew members in the small boat to shore. We all waited until Nemo himself set the first foot down. It was his right as the first man ever to land here. We got out after him, beached the boat, and climbed up a mountain in front of us. At the crest of this mountain, Nemo unfurled a black banner emblazoned with a gold N. Sinking it into the cold ground, he said, "On this day, I, Captain Nemo, take possession of this part of the globe."

"In whose name, Captain?" I asked.

He stared at me as if I had asked a very stupid question. "In my own name, Professor," he said with emphasis. "In my *own* name."

Returning to the *Nautilus,* we prepared to submerge once more. Outside, it was colder than ever. But inside the ship, it was warm and comfortable. Conseil and I joined Ned in our quarters. He was very moody lately, and it didn't take much to arouse his anger.

It must have been three o'clock in the morning when I was awakened by a violent shock. It knocked poor Conseil clean out of his bed and onto the metal floor. I sat bolt upright. The ship had struck something hard and rebounded sharply—that much I could tell. But what?

Dressing quickly now, my two friends and I entered the outside corridor. We hurried by the library, where we saw books scattered on the floor and chairs toppled. Shouts from near the captain's quarters filtered down the corridor. Outside Captain Nemo's door were some of his crew men, rubbing the sleep from their eyes. Then the door opened. Captain Nemo seemed to look through us. He was lost in thought. But the worry on his face made all of us, crew and passengers alike, very nervous.

"An accident?" I asked, unable to remain quiet a second longer.

"Yes," replied Nemo.

"Serious?"

"Perhaps."

"Is the *Nautilus* stranded?"

"Yes," he said once more.

"How?" I asked.

"A whole mountain of ice has turned over in the water," he answered me. "Sometimes, great icebergs are weakened from below by warmer water or heavy cracking. When that happens, they can turn completely over. One of them, in tumbling, struck the *Nautilus*. It then glided underneath our hull and raised it up. So, with a wall of icebergs both in front and in back of us, and solid ice just a few hundred feet above us, it appears we're— "

"Trapped!" I said, finishing the sentence for him. The word sent a shock wave of fear through us all. The captain anticipated my next question.

"We have a two-day supply of air left," he said. "Gentlemen, I propose we make the best of it. We'll have to dig our way out. And we must start now!"

After taking some soundings, Nemo located the least thick area of ice surrounding the ship. This area was below and just in front of the *Nautilus*. We would have to cut a hole thirty feet deep in the ice and as wide and long as the ship itself. And we would have to do this in forty-eight hours!

Each man aboard knew how serious our situation was. We split into two teams of diggers. One team worked outside while the other team rested inside. The outside team used pickaxes to chop and scrape and dig out the ice. They'd dig until their hands became too numb to hold the pickaxes. Then the other team relieved them. It was exhausting, backbreaking work. But there was no choice.

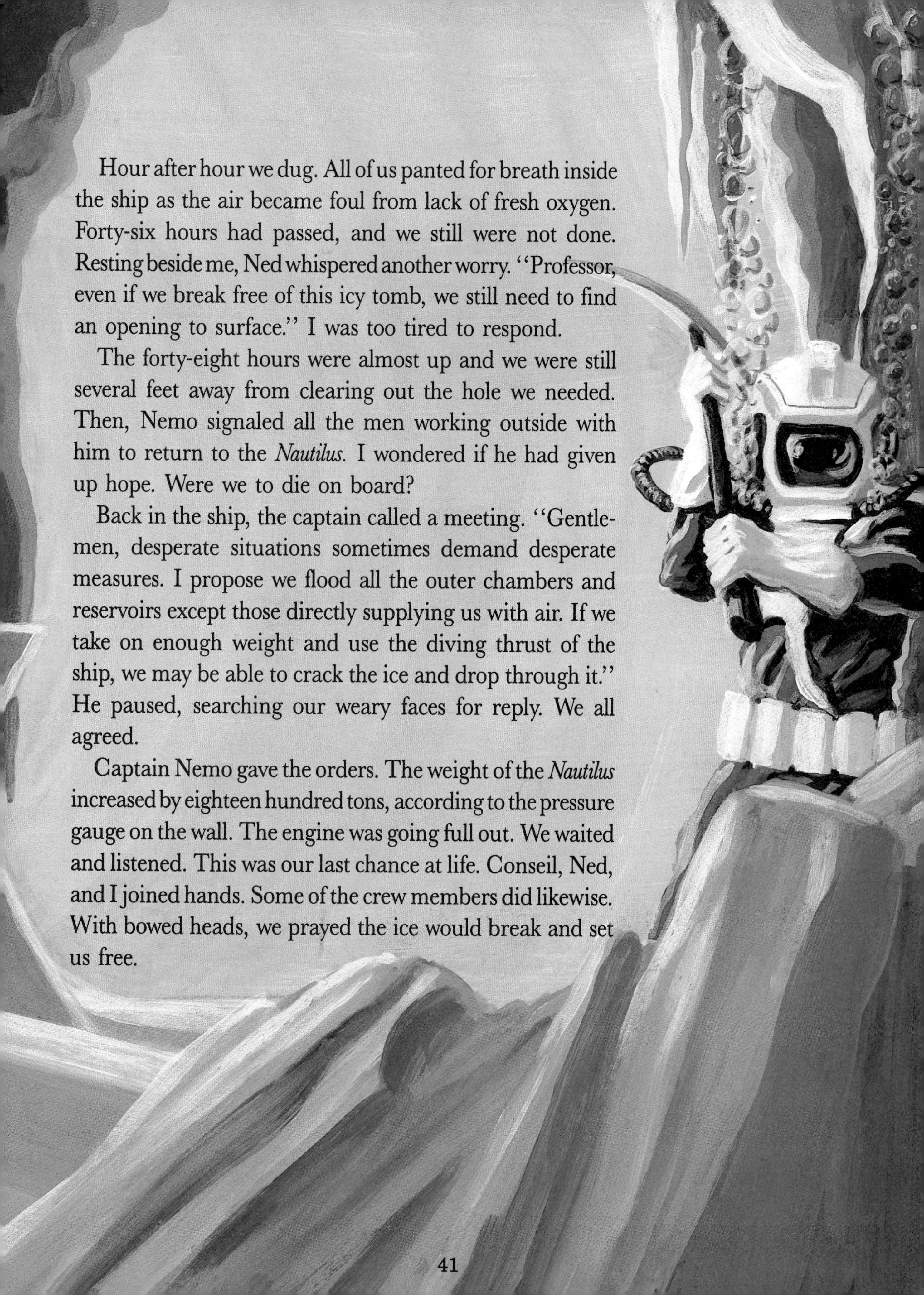

Hour after hour we dug. All of us panted for breath inside the ship as the air became foul from lack of fresh oxygen. Forty-six hours had passed, and we still were not done. Resting beside me, Ned whispered another worry. "Professor, even if we break free of this icy tomb, we still need to find an opening to surface." I was too tired to respond.

The forty-eight hours were almost up and we were still several feet away from clearing out the hole we needed. Then, Nemo signaled all the men working outside with him to return to the *Nautilus*. I wondered if he had given up hope. Were we to die on board?

Back in the ship, the captain called a meeting. "Gentlemen, desperate situations sometimes demand desperate measures. I propose we flood all the outer chambers and reservoirs except those directly supplying us with air. If we take on enough weight and use the diving thrust of the ship, we may be able to crack the ice and drop through it." He paused, searching our weary faces for reply. We all agreed.

Captain Nemo gave the orders. The weight of the *Nautilus* increased by eighteen hundred tons, according to the pressure gauge on the wall. The engine was going full out. We waited and listened. This was our last chance at life. Conseil, Ned, and I joined hands. Some of the crew members did likewise. With bowed heads, we prayed the ice would break and set us free.

Then, we heard a strange noise from below. The ice was cracking! The *Nautilus* pitched and dropped suddenly. It had broken through the ice. Immediately, Nemo ordered the pumps switched on. They soon forced out all the additional water we had taken on. Now we were moving forward, not downward. But there was no time to spare. We still had to find an opening in the surface.

Nemo stared at the ship's instruments. When one indicated the ice above us was no more than a couple of feet thick, he ordered the ship to ram upward at an angle. We would try to burst through, using the ship's steel spike. All of us grabbed onto the sides and prepared for the crash to come. The *Nautilus* sped closer and closer toward the ice above. Then the ship crashed into it, and we were thrown hard against the sides. But the sound of shattering ice told us the *Nautilus* had broken through. The hatches flew open, and all of us scrambled up on deck. For the first time in what seemed an eternity, we were breathing fresh air again, cold and clean.

During the next month, two incidents sharpened our desire to escape the *Nautilus* at the first opportunity. The first occurred in the waters off the Bahamas. The ship was cruising underwater at an easy clip when it suddenly stopped dead. Ned, Conseil, and I ran to the steering section and gasped at what we saw through the glass.

Before us was an immense octopus, staring at us with evil green eyes and flailing its eight tentacles. Horrible, blood-rimmed suction cups dotted the underside of each tentacle. From its ugly, beaked mouth emerged a tongue lined with what looked like pointed teeth. The beast must have weighed two or three tons, and its color changed very quickly from gray to reddish brown to black to gray again.

This monster was not alone, either. Six others, just as large, just as menacing, had entangled themselves in the ship's rudder and propeller. We had no choice but to surface and fight them off.

Armed with hatchets, and Ned with his harpoon, we waited for the main hatch to be opened. But as soon as it was released, a long tentacle shot down through the hatch. Captain Nemo cut it with his hatchet. But two other tentacles had wriggled down the ladder and wound around the waist of a crew man standing nearby. He was hoisted bodily into the air and out of the hole.

All of us bounded onto the deck. The seven monsters had attached their tentacles to various parts of the ship. One of them still held the crew man aloft. Nemo hacked fiercely at the tentacles holding his crew member in the air. He had almost succeeded in cutting through them when suddenly the octopus squirted a stream of black liquid that blinded him. By the time the captain recovered, the octopus had slid off the deck and back into the water, taking the crew man down with it.

The rest of us had been fighting and slashing the octopuses with our hatchets, lopping off tentacle after tentacle. Greasy blood oozing from the creatures' wounds slicked the deck, making our footing difficult. Ned Land was busy harpooning one octopus after another, striking at their green eyes. But he did not see one approach him from behind. Just before its beak was about to crunch Ned, Captain Nemo heaved his hatchet at the monster's eye. The octopus recoiled in pain. Blood poured from the deep gash in its eye. Then Ned took his harpoon and rammed it into the creature's heart. At this sight, the other five octopuses on deck slithered back into the sea.

As terrible as that incident was, the second was even more horrifying. A few miles off the Norwegian coastline, a ship of war had spotted and fired on the *Nautilus* after it surfaced. This other ship was a large, armored, two-decker ram, and it was steaming straight for the *Nautilus.* Cannon shots splashed around us. Nemo ordered everyone below.

"Captain, are you going to attack that ship?" I asked.

"Professor, I am going to sink it!" he bluntly replied. "And this time, Professor, you and your two comrades can witness its destruction."

I gathered with Conseil and Ned. In seconds, the *Nautilus* had dived a few feet and was heading directly toward the hull of the other ship. It was at battering speed when it struck just below the other ship's water line. The steel spike of the *Nautilus* ripped through the wooden underbelly of the other ship.

Nemo soon joined us. Together, the four of us watched as the ship began to sink. Water gushed into the hole left by the *Nautilus*' spike. Then, we saw them—the drowning crew members of the sinking ship. Soon, the struggle was over. The ship and its dead crew descended to the bottom of the sea forever.

Nemo left without uttering a word. Ned, Conseil, and I, however, were rooted to the spot. None of us could speak just then. We now knew why Nemo had ordered us below, had drugged us, and how that first crew member must have been wounded. The *Nautilus* had been ramming and sinking ships all along!

I spoke up first. "Tonight we escape!" I said hoarsely. "I will not spend another night on board this hellish ship!"

We set our plan. At ten o'clock that night, we'd go on deck, unbolt the small boat, and take our chances at sea in it. We were about twenty miles off the coast of Norway. Good weather or bad, calm sea or not, we were determined to leave. Nothing would stop us from trying.

In the minutes before ten, my heart was beating so loudly that I thought Ned and Conseil could hear it. Then the library clock struck ten times. It was now or never. Carrying a small bag each, we quietly slipped out of our quarters. As we passed by Captain Nemo's cabin, we could hear sobbing from within. But we ignored it and pressed on. We reached the main hatch and climbed out on deck. We went over to where the small boat was attached to the ship and started unbolting it, sitting inside the boat as we did so.

"Hurry!" I whispered. We were almost finished.

Then, all three of us heard shouts from within the *Nautilus*. "The whirlpool! The whirlpool!" they exclaimed.

In the darkness dimly lit by moonlight, we could barely see what the voices below meant. Just ahead of us was violently swirling water. The *Nautilus* was being sucked slowly but surely toward the outer rim of a huge whirlpool. We could now see the waves along its rim rise even higher and grow more violent.

"Hold on!" screamed Ned. The small boat had suddenly broken loose from the side of the ship. But Ned's warning came too late for me. I lost my grip and fell. My head struck something, and I blacked out.

I awoke in a fisherman's hut tucked along the Norwegian coast. Both Ned and Conseil were there with me. We clasped hands, happy to have escaped, grateful to be alive. How we managed this and made it to this kind fisherman's home, I cannot say.

Nor do I know what happened to the *Nautilus,* her crew, and her mysterious captain. Was "Nemo" even his real name? I still don't know. I only hope that if the *Nautilus* survived the whirlpool, her captain will eventually find in the depths of the sea the peace of mind and heart he could never find on land.